*The Universa*

# WHAT CHASE
# SEES IN SPACE

Laura Coy

Enchanted Moon Press
BOOKS FOR ALL PHASES OF LIFE

# DEDICATION

This, my first book, is dedicated to my precious family.
Matt, Tatem, and Chase- I love you to the moon and back.

# CONTENTS

# ACKNOWLEDGMENTS

This story originated from a dream I had years ago. I woke, went on with my life, but the dream stuck with me. It begged to be written. I couldn't have done it without the help of my village.

I want to thank my wonderful illustrator, Victoria Krueger, for bringing the cover, and each chapter, to life with her vision and talent.

I also want to thank my editor, Meg McIntyre, for her careful eyes and professional feedback.

A big thanks to my "Kid Test Group". These young readers were the first in my target age group to review the manuscript and offered valuable feedback. Luke Glover, Sam Goldberg, Hogan Leverett, thank you.

Finally, I want to thank my amazing friends and family for supporting me and believing in me. You've been by my side every step of the way. This book is yours too.

# 1 NEW TO TOWN

Chase looked through his closet with a frown and furrowed brows. A sigh escaped from deep within, one he didn't even know he was holding in. Chase had no idea what the kids in Maryland wore to school. *Would they dress the same way as his friends did in Georgia?* he wondered. *Were skate shirts cool or football jerseys? Did they wear preppy collared shirts or T-shirts?* Ugh, too much to think about. He threw on his favorite U.S. Navy T-shirt and a pair of jeans, hoping he would just blend in with the strangers.

This wasn't going to be easy. Chase grew up in a small town in Georgia. He'd lived there all ten years of his life. Everything about Georgia was familiar and easy for him- the friendly neighbors, his school, the teachers, and most importantly, his friends. Heck, he even missed his old dentist. Now, he was in a new house in a new neighborhood, about to start his first day of fifth grade at a new school.

"Why did we have to move to Maryland again?" he asked his family over breakfast. Mom looked down at her plate and took a deep breath. Chase didn't usually speak to his parents this way, but this morning, he was frustrated.

Dad was quick to answer. "Son, I've told you; I

accepted a new job. It was a once-in-a-lifetime opportunity. We're going to have a great life here. You just have to give it a chance and put your best foot forward. Think of it as a fresh start for our family. *The Magnussons Move to Maryland.*" Dad grinned at the other three Magnussons, who all looked anything but thrilled to start the day.

Chase's older sister, Tatem, mumbled something under her breath. If there was one person who was more rattled by this move than Chase, it was Tatem.

"Dad, we were perfectly happy in Georgia. I know you and Mom want us to give it a shot, but it's hard when all our friends are still there." Tatem looked down at her plate and moved her eggs around with her fork. "What if we don't find any new friends here? What if everyone here is different? What if they don't like us?"

Chase sighed and tried to pretend she was being overdramatic, but deep down, he was wondering the same thing himself. In fact, he was kind of hoping his older sister would have this all figured out. He'd hoped she would take the lead and show him how to navigate this big change.

Kids can be mean. Chase had witnessed this firsthand in Georgia. No one really picked on Chase, but he had seen what they were capable of. When new kids moved to his school, classmates would whisper and wonder, as if the new student couldn't see it all happening in front of them.

But now Chase was the new kid, and he would have to do this on his own. Tatem was starting her first day of seventh grade at the local middle school, Magothy Middle. And Chase- well, he was getting ready to start the first day of fifth grade at Broadneck Elementary.

Mom looked at the clock on the kitchen wall and gave the kids a big smile. "It's time!" she sang. Chase reluctantly grabbed his backpack and headed toward the door. Mom gave him a quick hug and handed him his lunchbox. He only had to walk to the corner to catch the bus, but to him, it felt like ten miles.

There were three other kids at the bus stop when Chase got there. None of them said anything. None of them even looked at him. Chase just stood there, looking at the cool, damp concrete below his feet. This was going to be tougher than he imagined.

One of the kids looked about his age, while the other two were younger. Chase didn't make eye contact with any of them but was hanging on every word they said. He gathered that the younger two were brother and sister. They had the same attitude when talking to each other that Chase and Tatem used when they were together. As much as they could get on each other's

nerves, Chase wished Tatem was there with him now. She

always knew what to say, how to start conversations.

Chase remained silent.

The bus rolled up and came to a stop. Chase hung

back and let the other kids go first. A soft line formed as

the kids entered one by one. Chase followed the other

kids onto the bus. The bus driver had a friendly smile, but

something about her told Chase she didn't tolerate nonsense. He picked an empty seat near the middle. He was glad no one sat next to him. He wanted a new friend, but he didn't really feel like talking. He sat silently and wondered why all buses smelled the same. It was the familiar scent of gasoline, rubber, old shoes, and possibly a rotten, half-eaten sandwich that was left on the bus the year before. Yuck.

Chase looked out the window and wondered if the bus would stop to pick up other kids before arriving at Broadneck Elementary. It did. The bus stopped once at a corner on the way out of the neighborhood, and then again on the street just outside of it. Grinning, giggling kids stepped onto the bus and took seats with ease.

As the bus took off down the main road toward his new school, Chase thought, *Here goes nothing.*

# 2 FIRST DAY OF SCHOOL

Chase sat cautiously in his assigned seat in his homeroom class. Three strangers shared his table, and they were all busy doing their own things. His fifth-grade teacher was cheerfully explaining something, but he was having a hard time paying attention. Chase pretended to work on his morning work but gazed around at the other kids. There were twenty-six kids in his class, and they *ALL* seemed to know each other. They were whispering about vacations, swim team, sleepovers, and camps. They were all smiling and laughing. Chase felt invisible.

He refocused on his morning work, a word search that his teacher created. It had all the students' names hidden in the puzzle. He looked for his name, trying to find a C and an H next to each other. He found his name in the bottom left, reading diagonally backwards. He looked at the list of other names to work on the next one. He read through the names in his head, thinking of his old classmates back in Georgia. He knew a Riley, a Carson, a Miguel, and a Dylan back at his old school. The other names on the roster were all new to him.

No one talked to him, and he really didn't have anything to say either. Chase couldn't wait for this day to be over.

Mrs. Ross seemed nice enough. She would be his teacher for homeroom, math, science, and social studies. Science was by far Chase's favorite subject. He loved trying new experiments. He had done one last year on heat. Chase started daydreaming about his experiment— filling out the entry form, working on it at his old house, presenting it at the showcase at school, and taking home the big blue first place ribbon.

Chase was startled when Mrs. Ross clapped her hands five times to get the class's attention. The class clapped back five times in the same rhythm. Class had officially started. Mrs. Ross gave a rundown of what to expect throughout the year. They would start with the astronomy unit. *Of course*, thought Chase, the pit in his stomach growing bigger. That was one topic in science he knew nothing about. Chase didn't know much about it because he didn't care about it. Astronomy sounded boring. Who cares about planets and stars and moons that are thousands of miles away? You can't visit them. You can't touch them. Chase was into the kind of science that you could get your hands on. This was the one topic he had zero interest in. Could things get worse?

Yes. When they switched classrooms to go to their language arts teacher, he got knocked around the halls like a ping-pong ball. It was like he was invisible. People ran right into him, and when he leaned down to pick up the book he dropped, he was practically trampled by a herd of bigger fifth graders. At his old school, he had anxiously awaited the day he would be in fifth grade. King of the School. But here, he felt as small as the newest kindergartener.

*Glory Pete*, Chase thought. He would have to remember to walk toward the back of the pack tomorrow. At least the school day was almost over. He couldn't wait to get back home to people who knew and loved him.

Chase had almost made it through the day. In fact, he had left the school building and was walking across the grassy field toward the buses when he heard a thud. Chase whipped his head around to see three girls who looked familiar from lunch. They were all giggling and leaning into each other. It didn't take long for Chase to see what they were giggling at. There was another girl crouched in the grass and dirt, trying to pick up her books. Why were those girls laughing at her? Chase thought about going back to help the girl gather her books. Then the three girls saw Chase staring and one of them asked, "What are you looking at?"

Chase turned and walked toward his bus. He wasn't one for confrontation. But he had only taken about three steps when his conscience got the best of him. He was fed up with the day and had nothing to lose. He stopped, turned around, and faced the girls. He said, "I was looking at you being rude to someone who probably didn't deserve it."

Chase noticed that the little girl who had dropped her books was nowhere to be found. He scanned the field for her, but no luck. The three giggly, mean girls just tossed their hair and took off in the other direction. Chase turned and headed for his bus, ready to get home and leave this place behind.

He had just settled into a seat near the front when someone came and joined him. Chase looked up to see another boy about his age squished in beside him. The boy managed a "Hey man," but then turned to talk with others around him on the bus. At least he had acknowledged Chase.

Then it happened. Chase watched her climb the steps onto the bus right in front of him. It was one of the three girls he had just confronted on the field. She caught his eye and then let out her breath dramatically as she rolled her eyes. She started down the aisle to the back of the bus then stopped. She turned around and said, "Loser," loud enough for everyone to hear.

Great. The whole point of the day was to make friends, not enemies. Chase put his backpack on his lap and rested his head against the cool window. He looked out the clear glass, wondering what his friends were up to back in Georgia.

After what seemed like the longest ride ever, Chase's bus stopped near his new house. Chase squeezed past the kid next to him and walked down the aisle. Just before he walked down the steps, the bus driver said, "My name is Ms. Linda. If anyone messes with you, you just let me know." Then she gave him a slow nod up and down. Chase understood and mumbled, "Thank you, ma'am." He walked down the steps, out into the fresh air, and made his way home with his head down.

When Chase walked through his garage door, his mom was there with another big smile. "How was your day, sweetie? It wasn't nearly as bad as you had thought, now was it?" she asked. She walked toward him with a plate of warm cookies.

"Yes. Yes, it was bad. In fact, Mom, it was terrible. I don't know any of those kids and they don't want to get to know me," Chase explained.

Mom came in for a hug, but Chase didn't feel like one. As much as those warm cookies were calling his name, his desire to escape the day was more powerful. He threw his backpack in the corner of the living room, ran upstairs to his room, and shut the door. He needed some alone time. Chase threw himself on his beanbag chair and grabbed the video game controller that was tucked in the side pocket. He escaped his dismal reality for an hour as he entered the world of Fortnite.

Later that evening, once Tatem was home from school

too, Mom called everyone down for dinner. She had a bell that she kept right above the sink. She rang it three times as she called out for the family to come to the table. Chase's two dogs, Brinkley and Bogey, had learned what that bell meant. As the humans gathered around for dinner, the dogs joined in too with wagging tails and smiles!

"Roses and thorns and something you learned," Mom chimed as they sat down for dinner. They had a family tradition of going over a good part of their day, a bad part of their day, and—because Mom was once a teacher—she also made them share something they learned. The family of four went in birth order, youngest to oldest, so Chase always had to share first.

Tonight, Chase just wanted to skip his turn, but he knew that wasn't an option. He used his fork to separate his peas from his potatoes. He hated when anything touched on his plate. Chase figured he might as well just get it over with so he could enjoy the rest of his meal. He cleared his throat. "My rose is that I am not at school right now, so that's a good thing. My thorn is the new school and all the people in it. They're awful. And what I learned today is that I really miss my old friends. Next." Chase looked down at his plate.

Chase's mom made a little noise in her throat that she did when she was disappointed or worried. Chase didn't look up from his plate but could tell that his mom and dad were trading concerned looks across the table. He didn't want to upset his parents. He knew that they wanted him to be happy. What they didn't know was how hard it was to switch schools and lose all your friends.

It was now Tatem's turn. She loved the spotlight.

"Okay. Well, my rose is that there's a really cute

boy in my math class. I think he likes me. My thorn is that another girl was wearing the same shirt as me—awkward! And what I learned is that Chase is actually smarter than he looks. I agree with him. Our old school and friends back in Georgia are much better than what we have to deal with here."

Chase looked up at Tatem and she gave him a little wink. She was always trying to look after him and this was no exception. It felt good to know that someone had his back.

The rest of dinner consisted of Mom and Dad reassuring Tatem and Chase that it was going to get better. They just needed to give it time and have open minds. Chase continued to push peas around his plate with his fork, waiting until he was excused from the table.

"Come on, kiddos, everyone needs to eat at least a

few bites. Tomorrow is a new day. Each day is a fresh start." That was one of Mom's favorite quotes. She was always telling them some inspirational quote. Chase imagined her having a library of books full of quotes sitting in her brain, waiting for the perfect situation. This made him laugh to himself. He decided to cut his mom some slack. He piled a forkful of peas into his mouth and gave her a half smile. That was all she needed. Mom's shoulders dropped as the stress released from her body.

"Thank you for trying, buddy. I know this can't be easy," Mom said sympathetically. Chase finished his dinner, and he did feel a smidge better.

Chase was excused from the table. On his way to take his plate to the sink, he tossed a nugget to each dog, who quickly gulped them down. Just as he was about to climb the stairs to get to the solitude of his room, Dad called him back.

"Oh, buddy, I forgot to tell you that there's a back-to-school picnic this Friday evening at your school. Your mom and I will get to meet your teachers and some of the other parents. I'm looking forward to it. The email from your school says they'll have all sorts of activities for you kids. It should be a fun night," he said with a big smile.

Chase tried to put on a pleasant face. "Okay, Dad."

He turned and ran upstairs to finally escape the day. When he got to his room, Chase shut the door, as if he were separating himself from the day he'd endured. He didn't even feel like playing video games. He went to his sink to wash his face and brush his teeth. He plopped a big gob of toothpaste on his neon green toothbrush and moved the toothbrush back and forth and up and down. When he had finished, he looked at himself in the mirror.

Chase looked exactly as he had when he lived in Georgia just weeks ago. His dirty blonde, straight hair swept across his forehead. His dark brown eyes stared back as he examined himself. He leaned into the mirror as he stroked his ivory cheeks. He looked like the same Chase. But everything else felt completely different.

# 3 BASKETBALL

The week went by like a turtle stuck in mud. It did get a

little better for Chase on Friday. The other kids were

starting to acknowledge him, and he even found one guy

that seemed kind of nice. Jackson had seen that Chase

was a pretty good athlete during P.E. class throughout the

week. So on Friday, Jackson called him over to be on his

basketball team.

"Hey, I don't know your name, but you wanna play on our team?" Jackson had asked.

"Sure," Chase replied casually. He didn't want to seem too eager. But Chase noticed that this was the same boy who had sat with him on the way home from school on the first day. Chase remembered how the boy had said hi to him and not just ignored him like everyone else that day.

They played well together. They were just getting into a rhythm when one of the other boys, Nick, called Jackson out for traveling. Chase couldn't believe it. There was no way that Jackson had run without dribbling the ball. He was dribbling the whole time! Chase looked at the other kids to see if they would speak up. Nothing. Jackson tried to defend himself, saying that he knew he was dribbling, but Nick was insistent. Chase kept looking to the other guys to speak up. When no one did, Chase found his voice.

"Dude, he was definitely dribbling. Let it go and let's keep playing. We don't want to waste any of our P.E. time arguing."

Once the words were out of Chase's mouth, he immediately wondered what the backlash would be. The last time he spoke up for what was right was in the school field on the way to buses. He remembered how that had turned out for him.

But surprisingly, Nick shrugged his shoulders and threw the ball back to Jackson to play. Alright. This had gone better than expected.

Before they knew it, the teacher blew his whistle.

"Time to line up. Get all the balls put away and line up in number order for your teacher," Mr. Capes called out.

Chase knew most kids hated number order. He knew this because he himself had hated number order at his old school. He just wanted to stand next to his friends. But here, he kind of appreciated number order. It gave him a place to feel included without having to worry about the fact that he didn't have many friends here.

The kids at Broadneck Elementary seemed to all know one another. It reminded Chase of how he felt at his old school in Georgia. He had known most of the kids since preschool. They had been in play groups together as toddlers, shared class parties, been on sports teams together, and spent the weekends hanging out too. Chase tried telling himself that he would get there someday with the kids here in Maryland. It would just take some time.

The school day dragged on until it was time for recess. Chase headed out in number order with the rest of the class. He was daydreaming as he took in the fresh, autumn air. He was guessing he would pass the free time by just walking around by himself when he heard someone shout his name.

Jackson came running over. "Hey man, you wanna pick up that basketball game where we left off? The other guys are in too."

"Sure!" Chase said. This time he didn't care if his excitement was noticeable.

Playing sports always made Chase forget his problems. They had almost twenty minutes to forget about schoolwork and just have fun on the court. When Mrs. Ross blew her whistle for the kids to line up, the guys all said good job to each other and bumped knuckles—Chase included.

# 4 BACK-TO-SCHOOL PICNIC

Friday evening finally rolled around, and Chase knew

what that meant: the dreaded back-to-school night. These

things were always so boring. His mom and dad were

eager and excited to meet other parents at the school.

Chase couldn't understand it. He just wanted to get the

night over with. He was hoping they'd get home in time

for him to play video games with his friends in Georgia.

They loaded into the family SUV and headed out.

All four of the Magnussons were going to this event.

Tatem kept saying she didn't understand why she had to

go. She didn't even go to elementary school. Chase had to

admit he agreed with her. It was bad enough that he had

to go. He couldn't imagine how boring it would be for his

sister.

The SUV pulled down the lane that led to the

school. It was packed. Cars were parked along the sides

of the street and every parking spot looked filled. Dad

scanned the lot. "Oh hey, I think I see someone leaving

now. We'll grab that spot." He slowly pulled in behind a

car that was backing out. As their car turned into the

spot, Chase caught a glimpse of the people in the car that

was leaving. It was that girl from his bus—the mean girl.

Chase had heard someone call her name at recess. Her

name was Janessa. At least he wouldn't have to deal with

running into her tonight. *Good riddance, Janessa,* thought Chase.

The family of four walked toward the sea of tents. Tatem was texting someone on her phone. Chase was looking at his feet as he walked. Mom was walking confidently ahead with a look of purpose. Dad was nodding at people he didn't even know and smiling.

The teachers greeted the families and showed the parents to the "Parent Tent," while all the kids were shuffled off to the back playground. Chase kept his eyes on the ground and went toward the huge mass of kids. Tatem wandered off to try to find some friends her age. Chase just followed the group of kids, not knowing exactly what the evening would bring.

The volunteers had set up stations for all the students. It kind of looked like a carnival, but without the best part: the rides. One station was painting little clay flowerpots. You could make a friendship bracelet at a different station. You could try to knock over bottles with a bean bag at another. One tent had a float or sink test. At yet another station, you could decorate a cookie. Nothing seemed to interest Chase until he saw a line of three telescopes set up at the last station. He also saw a familiar face: Mrs. Ross.

He made his way over and listened as his science teacher explained that Jupiter would be visible within minutes, just as the sun went down. Chase was thinking that if he wanted to continue getting good grades, he'd better figure out what all this astronomy was about. He paused and listened as his teacher explained that Jupiter has moons, just like Earth. She checked the telescope as she talked.

Finally, after what felt like an eternity, Mrs. Ross told the students that the sun had gone down enough.

She could see Jupiter through the lens. The kids lined up behind the three telescopes, ready to take a peek. Some were pushing and cutting in front of others. Chase was in no rush and hung toward the back.

When it was finally Chase's turn, he put his eye up to it. *Huh?* he thought. Everything was blurry. He looked over at the kid next to him, who was looking through another telescope. That kid had one eye squeezed shut. Chase tried it again, this time with one eye wide open, looking through the lens, and his other eye squeezed shut.

"Coooooool," whispered Chase. He could see Jupiter. It was a big, round, yellow object in the night sky. He looked at it for a while, moving the focus knob back and forth. He could see thick stripes and swirls forming a pattern across Jupiter's surface. At this point, most of the kids had gotten bored and moved on to other stations.

Chase thought it wouldn't hurt anything to keep looking a little longer. No one was behind him in line.

Chase slowly moved the telescope to the right of Jupiter. He found something. *This must be one of Jupiter's moons,* he thought to himself. He turned the focus knob a bit and the image of the moon got bigger and clearer.

Chase was looking intently through the viewfinder when he saw the first flash of motion. "What the heck?" he said out loud. He looked back to make sure no one had heard him and then looked again. Oh yeah, that was definite movement on Jupiter's moon. Like shadows bouncing and dancing on the surface. Chase stood straight up and looked around. Only Mrs. Ross was left at the station with him. The other kids had all moved on to other activities.

"Um, Mrs. Ross, I have a question," Chase said unsurely.

"Sure Chase. I'm glad to see you over here with such interest. What can I help you with?" Mrs. Ross asked.

"Well, is there any documented life on Jupiter's moon?" Chase asked, knowing his question sounded ridiculous.

"Oh, I'm afraid not, Chase. We have yet to discover life on any other planet, much less a planet's moon. We need water, oxygen, plants, and animals to survive. Scientists just haven't found evidence of any of that in outer space," Mrs. Ross answered. Chase liked her. She didn't make him feel stupid for asking that question.

He moved over to the next telescope. Maybe it was just something quirky with the one he was using first. Maybe he didn't really see any movement at all.

Chase positioned the telescope and put his eye to the viewfinder. He squinted the other eye shut and started turning the focus knob, zooming in on Jupiter. Then he turned the telescope ever so slightly to the right. Again, he saw Jupiter's moon. He inhaled abruptly. This time, he didn't just see shadows; he saw aliens! Shadows of creatures, with two legs and lots of arms, caught him by surprise.

Chase pushed his chair out and ran from the station.

"Chase! Is everything okay?" Mrs. Ross called after him. But Chase didn't stick around to answer. He needed to get out of there. What in the world?! Chase considered that he might be losing his mind. Maybe the stress of the move and new school had pushed him over the edge. There was absolutely no way that there were real aliens on Jupiter's moon. Mrs. Ross had said it herself; no life had been confirmed anywhere but Earth. But Chase could not get the image out of his mind. They were like people, but different. He was replaying what he saw in his head when he walked right into one of the guys he'd played basketball with at recess earlier in the day.

# 5 CARNIVAL GAMES

"Oh, sorry man. You okay?" Chase asked the kid he had just run into.

"Yeah, I'm fine. I'm Nick by the way."

"I'm Chase. I just moved here. I think we played basketball together today," Chase reminded him.

"Oh yeah.  Wanna go with me to the rubber duck

station?" Nick asked, with a glint of mischief in his eye.

Chase was happy to have someone to hang out with and grateful for the opportunity to get his mind off what he had just seen through the telescope. The boys started walking in the direction of one of the only tents with prizes.

Nick looked like he had been at the picnic for a while. His cheeks were rosy from running around and his skin was dewy from the warm evening.

"You see," explained Nick, a little out of breath, "all you have to do is pick a rubber duck from the pond. If it has a red dot under it, you win."

That didn't sound too hard, until they reached the station and Chase saw how many ducks were in the pond. There must have been a hundred! There was no way anyone had a chance to win with that many ducks in play.

one they picked, and then waited for my own turn. This is my third prize from the same game."

So Nick had been to that station before. He had lied right to that lady's face. Not only had he been there once before, but he had already won the game twice! Chase knew Nick was proud of his winning skills, but Chase didn't like it. Chase had always felt if you had to cheat to win, it really wasn't a win at all. Even if you did walk away with three stuffed animals.

They got to where Nick's parents were standing and talking with a group of other parents. Nick tossed his stuffed animal in a pile at his mom's feet with the other two.

His eager eyes set in on Chase. "Alright Chase, now it's your turn. You just need to pick a duck that has a cowboy hat, nurses' uniform, or blue necklace. You're guaranteed a win. Let's go back." Nick started off ahead of him.

Chase didn't want to upset Nick. He was the only classmate that night that took the time to hang out with him. But Chase also didn't feel right cheating. He needed an out, and fast. Just then, he saw Tatem walking by with another girl her age.

"Oh, that's my sister. Sorry Nick, I've gotta run. I'll catch you at school on Monday," Chase said as he ran off toward Tatem.

"C'mon man, just one try," Nick yelled to Chase. But Chase had no intention of looking back. He had an out with Tatem, and he was taking it. Chase was relieved to finally be going home.

# 6 OPERATION INVESTIGATION

Later that evening, when Chase and his family got home, his mind was back on what he had seen through the telescope. Chase knew that he saw shadows and aliens, but his eyes must have been deceiving him. It couldn't have been real. His teacher and classmates looked through the same exact telescopes and they didn't see anything strange. Chase was anxious to do some investigating. "Dad, can I borrow your computer for a little bit?" Chase asked.

"Sure, buddy. Gonna play some games?" his dad replied.

"Yeah, something like that," Chase said as he grabbed the laptop.

Chase ran up the stairs to his room in record time. He got settled on his bed, put the computer on his lap, and pulled up a search engine. His fingers typed out the words LIFE ON JUPITER MOON. His heart raced as he anticipated the results. What if something did come up confirming what he had seen through the telescope earlier that evening? Chase needed to know for sure if there was life out there.

He hadn't told anyone that he had seen
movement through his telescope. No way. As if being the
new kid at school—and new to an entire state—didn't
make him stand out enough. The last thing he wanted to
do was isolate himself even more. But why would *he* be
the only one able to see this?

He hit ENTER and his search began. He scrolled
through the articles that popped up. Ugh. Everything he

clicked just confirmed what his teacher had told him. There was no way there was life on one of Jupiter's moons. He did find out that Jupiter had a bunch of them. Man, space was enormous.

Chase tried wording his search a little differently. He put in LIFE IN SPACE. Now, this search brought up a bunch of bizarre stuff. But everything said that it was unconfirmed, meaning there was no proven, scientific truth to it.

Just as Chase was giving up hope on his search, he heard his Xbox ding. Hmm. He walked over and saw that there was a request to play with someone named "Jaxman." Chase didn't know anyone named Jaxman. He thought about all his friends, seeing if their names might be similar to Jaxman. Aha! Maybe it was Jackson, the kid who had asked him to play basketball at school. Chase used his controller to click on the profile. He accepted the request, and within seconds, they were playing together. Well, their avatars were playing together in a virtual reality, but hey, it was a start.

Chase and Jackson helped each other navigate through the rooms and levels. Between strategizing, they talked a little about the back-to-school picnic. Jackson had to leave early to get to his brother's baseball game, so that's why Chase never ran into him. Chase didn't tell him about Nick. He didn't want to sound like a snitch. They played for almost an hour before Chase heard a knock on his door.

"Hey, bud. It's time to turn those video games off. You've been playing for almost two hours."

Chase didn't want to stop. He also knew the truth. He hadn't been playing video games for two hours. One of those hours was spent searching for life in space.

But he couldn't explain that to his dad, so he just agreed.

"Alright, Dad. I'm getting off now." Then Chase said into his headset, "Jackson, I've gotta go. Maybe we could play again tomorrow."

"Yeah, just hit me up tomorrow." They both shut their games down and turned in for the night.

Chase lay in bed and thought again about what he had seen through the telescope at the picnic. He wasn't making this up. He knew what he saw. The internet was no help. Chase knew he had to figure this out for himself. And he had an idea of just how he was going to do it.

# 7 THE NEXT STEPS

When Chase woke up the next morning, he was ready to put his plan into action. What he needed was his own telescope to see if he was fooled or if there really was life out in space. And, if there was life out in space, he wanted to know more.

It was Saturday, so Tatem was still sound asleep. That girl could sleep 'til noon on the weekends. That was probably best. She had a way of knowing when he was up to something. Like the time when Chase was a toddler and she knew things were a little too quiet. Tatem had gone downstairs and found Chase coloring on his legs with a magic marker. Luckily he had used a pack of washable markers, so it wasn't a big deal. In fact, Tatem had even helped clean him up before Mom had a chance to catch him. But this was different. Chase wasn't ready to tell anyone anything about what he had seen through the telescope, even his own sister.

"Good morning, sweetie," his mom sang as Chase walked into the kitchen. Time to work on his plan.

"Hey, Mom. I've been thinking. I really enjoyed looking through the telescope last night with my teacher, Mrs. Ross. She said our unit on astronomy this year is pretty intense. She even mentioned that we might want to get our own telescopes. I really want to be on top of my schoolwork and try for even better grades this year. Do

you think maybe we could consider buying a telescope?"

Chase asked in a polite, sweet voice. He gave his mom the

eyes—not full-on puppy dog eyes, but just enough.

"Oh, honey. I don't know about a telescope. I

don't even know how much those things cost, but I'm

sure they're not cheap." She turned to put the dishes away

and stopped. "Although, I am glad you're taking an interest in something. You haven't been excited about much since the move. And it is for school. Hmm. Let me think about it for a bit and talk to your father when he gets home from golf."

Chase tried to conceal his excitement, but a little, "Yesss!" squeaked out as he brought his fist in. His mom didn't need to know the real reason why he wanted a telescope. He just needed to convince her to get him one, and he was off to a good start.

That afternoon when Chase's father got home, Chase gently reminded his mom that she might have something to discuss with him. She winked and told him she would get to it. But she told Chase he first had to go outside and get some fresh air and play for a bit.

Chase used to love to go out and play. He would

grab a football or basketball from the garage and make his way out onto the driveway. Within seconds, his buddies in the cul-de-sac would mosey over and they would all start playing. It was effortless. It was easy. It was fun. Nothing about his new neighborhood was effortless, easy, or fun.

Chase didn't know one kid on his block. Heck, he didn't even really know what the kids at the bus stop looked like since he had kept his head down most of the time. Chase grabbed a tennis ball and his racquet out of the bin in his garage and went out to the driveway. He started bouncing the ball against the cement and pushing it back down with his racquet.

It felt weird being out there all alone. Chase missed the familiar friends, sights, and sounds from his old neighborhood. He was daydreaming of his old neighbor's dog and how she always tried to steal his tennis ball when he heard a cheerful voice.

"Hey Chase! I didn't know this was your house. Mind if I join you?" It was Jackson, the boy he met in P.E. class and played video games with last night.

"Sure, I'll grab you a racquet," Chase said, trying to play it cool and not sound nearly as excited as he really was.

The boys hit the ball back and forth for a while, talking easily. Jackson asked Chase how long he had lived there. Chase asked Jackson if he played on any sports teams. Jackson told him about a cool trail in the woods that led to a fort. Chase told him about his video game collection. Chase was having a good time—an effortless, easy, fun time with his new friend, Jackson. Things were looking up, for now.

# 8 THE TELESCOPE

Chase and Jackson spent the afternoon playing in and out of Chase's house and all around the neighborhood. They were both surprised when Chase's mom called him in for dinner. Where had the day gone? They were having so much fun they didn't even notice it was starting to get dark. Jackson left, telling Chase he would see him tomorrow.

Chase walked into the house in a glow of sweat and happiness. He stopped in the bathroom to wash his hands and then joined his family at the table. It was hamburger night. "Yesss!"

Chase's father started the conversation. "So, Chase, Mom tells me you are interested in astronomy. I think that's actually pretty cool. I studied a bit of astronomy myself in college. I used to have this quirky professor who would have us sit on rolling chairs with our telescopes so we could turn our bodies 360 degrees to see the whole galaxy. Oh, those were good ol' times. We even got to go up into the planetarium on campus. Man, you could see everything from up there."

Chase stopped his father before he drifted even further down memory lane. "Boy, Dad, that sounds like a blast. Do you think maybe we could get a telescope so we could do that stuff from home?" Chase put on the same sweet face and puppy dog eyes he'd used with his mom.

"I can do you one better, buddy," Chase's father said excitedly. "Believe it or not, I still have my old telescope from college. It's somewhere down in the basement. I think it's still in a box from the move. Heck, it's been in a box for almost fifteen years."

Chase couldn't believe what he was hearing. All the convincing he thought he would have to do to get a telescope, and there had been one in his basement this whole time! He couldn't wait to get down there and find it.

Chase and his father finished dinner quickly. Then they rushed downstairs to begin the search for the box with the telescope in it. There were so many boxes still stacked up and unopened from the move. The storage room smelled a little musty and the lights weren't that bright. It was tough to find the right box. "No, not that one," his dad said as he pushed a box to the side. "No, not that one either. We really should have labeled these better."

Chase was peeking through corners of boxes, but really didn't know how a telescope would fit in a box in the first place. The one he looked through at school was on a big tripod. He was trying to remember just what it looked like when his dad yelled, "Aha! Here she is!"

Chase's dad pulled out an old, dusty, silver and black tube. Then he pulled out something that looked like metal feet. "She's gonna need a little TLC, but I think this will work just fine."

Chase and his dad carried the telescope parts upstairs to the living room. Together, they worked very carefully to clean the outer body of the telescope, as well as the fragile lens. Then they took the pieces up to Chase's room. Chase had a big window to the left of his bed. Without even discussing it, both Chase and his dad knew this would be the perfect home for his telescope. They started the assembly together.

It didn't take long at all. In fact, it was perfect timing because the sun was just starting to set when Chase's telescope was ready. He was anxious to get started, but he didn't want to look through it with his dad watching him. This was something he had to do on his own. His dad knew him too well and he would surely know something was up by Chase's facial expressions. Chase just kind of stood there for a moment.

Like he was reading his mind, Chase's dad said, "Well buddy, I'm gonna let you figure this thing out on your own. She's yours now. I'm happy to pass it down to you. Call me up if you need any help, but I have a pretty good feeling you'll master this in no time."

"And Chase," his dad added. "Be careful. Space is a very mysterious place. It has the power to pull you in." With that, Dad walked out and shut the door to Chase's room.

# 9 LOOKING THROUGH THE LENS

Chase stood frozen in his room. What did his dad mean

by that? Did his dad know what he had seen when he first

looked through the telescope at school? Although these

were pressing questions, he pushed them aside. He

couldn't wait to look through the old telescope that was

now set up in his room.

Chase walked toward it. He pulled his desk chair

over to his window, took a seat, and positioned himself behind the telescope, which was in front of his big window. The sky was now a dark indigo blue. Soon it would be black. There were some trees and houses out front, but above all that was the big open night sky. There was not a cloud to be seen. Butterflies danced in Chase's belly.

For a moment, Chase worried that it might not be a good idea to look. He pushed the chair back, got up, and paced his room. Did he really want to continue this?

Chase jumped up on his bed and buried his face in his pillow. He felt alone. He felt scared. He felt different.

He rolled over and looked up at his ceiling. He closed his eyes and looked within. He made a mental list of the pros and cons of looking through the telescope.

He thought about the worst-case scenario and the best-case scenario. He thought about how he could have some cool superpowers and he thought about how this could make him even more different than everyone else.

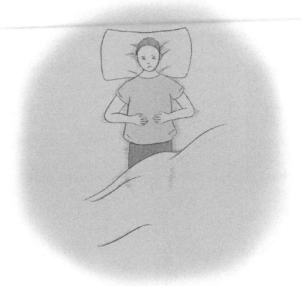

He never felt different in Georgia. He could be himself and no one ever challenged him. This was the first time he had really been confronted with a dilemma.

Chase decided he was going to tackle it head-on. If he didn't look through the telescope, he would always wonder. He believed that he could handle anything he saw.

Chase took a deep breath and put one eye up to the viewfinder. He squinted his other eye and began turning the focus knob. He could see some blurry objects—giant orbs of unfocused light. Then he turned the telescope to the bright light that he knew as Jupiter. Nothing. He turned it a bit farther to the right and saw its moon. Bam!

Chase held his breath as he tried to digest what he was seeing. Everything he had read on the computer said there was no life in space. No life meant no one to build houses, cars, buildings, or anything else for that matter. But he was seeing all of this through the telescope.

Chase could see blurred objects buzzing around.

He squinted harder and turned the focus knob a smidge more. He could now see a bit clearer. He leaned in. *What in the world?*

# 10 JUPITER'S MOON

Through the viewfinder, Chase saw a far-off land full of life. No, seriously! There were people, or aliens, or space creatures, or whatever you want to call them, just going about their business on this moon. Chase took it all in, not even realizing he was holding his breath. He gasped a little and let out some air, then took a few deep breaths to steady himself.

The creatures he saw were kind of like humans, but the biggest discrepancy was that these creatures had four arms, two stacked on each side of their bodies. Long wavy arms, like an octopus. Each creature's skin was a different color of the rainbow. One's skin looked like a mix between the color of a pastel lavender Easter egg and a grape taffy candy. Another's skin reminded Chase of a robin's egg, the loveliest color of baby blue. Some of these creatures had smooth skin, while others had textures woven in—bumps and scales. Chase couldn't stop staring. This was unbelievable. He watched the creatures move about in big, long strides.

Just then, a cross between a car and a plane whizzed by. One of the creatures casually jumped in and took off. The vehicle looked like a fancy race car that went superfast and hovered over the ground, not on it. Chase remembered the time he had ridden in his uncle's

Corvette last summer. He had never felt a car take off so fast. The ride got faster and faster each time his uncle shifted the gears. That was nothing compared to how fast this vehicle took off. Chase wondered about gravity and how these creatures walked on the ground, but the vehicles were inches above it. The ground itself was coated in a thick layer of what looked like—were those rainbow sprinkles? This was amazing!

Chase's eyes followed the sprinkled road to the sidewalks. He noticed the buildings next. There were tall towers and some short storefronts, just like in cities he had visited here on Earth. But these buildings were all bright neon colors, made of something that looked like Play-Doh. The surfaces looked smooth and rubbery, with no apparent shape. Each house was brighter in color than the next. These colors were indescribable, colors Chase never knew existed. He had never seen colors so vibrant.

The plants were the next thing Chase noticed. His jaw was pretty much on the floor when he took it in. The trees and flowers were astoundingly gorgeous and alive. Each plant had bright, kelly green leaves and stems. The actual flower heads were enormous with huge petals. Then Chase noticed something. The flower heads were moving. Chase watched as two flowers dipped into each other, almost like they were having a conversation. The flowers had markings that resembled eyes and mouths. They bounced around, so joyful, as if they were sharing a joke.

Chase noticed something whiz by behind the talking flowers. His first thought was that it was one of those plane race cars. But then he saw the track. This was a roller-coaster! His eyes found the line of cars and followed it as it zipped and slung around the track.

Chase loved roller-coasters. He thought about the

mega-coaster he had ridden back in Georgia. He usually tried to assess situations, stay in control, and remain calm. Not on roller-coasters! That was one of the only times Chase gave up control and just let the ride take over. He delighted in the thrill of not knowing when the car would lurch forward on the track. He loved soaking in the view as the car climbed the tall track up the first hill. He always threw his hands up in the air as the car flew down, feeling as close to flying as he ever had.

The creatures on the roller-coaster he was seeing now seemed so calm. He watched as it slowed down for passengers to get off. They walked off in different directions, as if they had a purpose and somewhere to go. Chase watched the next group of passengers board, pull down their harnesses, and take off. It was all so common and casual for these creatures. There were no arms in the air or high-pitched screams. Chase watched them ride until the cars slowed down for departure again. Wait, that wasn't where they got off before, was it? This location was on the other side of the town. *Oh my gosh!* Chase thought. This wasn't just a roller-coaster; this was their transportation to get around town! Brilliant!

Between the roller-coaster, the race car spaceships zipping around, the creatures striding to and fro with their four arms, and the brilliant colors of the town, Chase was completely overwhelmed. He was considering closing his eyes and checking his sanity when something—or someone—caught his eye.

She was purple, with four arms, but something about her seemed familiar. Chase looked closer at her. Maybe it was the way her eyes looked. Maybe it was the way she was walking. She looked happy, but vulnerable. Chase couldn't take his eyes off her. He felt a deep connection to her that he could not explain.

Just then, three other creatures came around the corner laughing. They looked at her and then looked at each other. Their laughter got louder, and their pace picked up. They walked right toward the girl without slowing down one bit. They ran smack into her. Startled, she fell to the ground as they took off running. A pang of sadness, anger, and hurt hit Chase like a brick. It was not too long ago that he was in the same situation in the halls of his new school. He remembered how angry he was. He remembered how lonely and embarrassed he felt. He also remembered the schoolyard on his first day of school. His heart ached as he thought about the mean girls laughing at their innocent classmate.

The purple space creature pulled herself up and dusted herself off. She reclaimed the books that had fallen with her and held them close to her chest. She took a deep breath and looked down at the sprinkled street below her feet. Then, ever so slowly, she raised her head and looked directly into Chase's eyes.

was *he* able to see all of this? Could anyone else see what he could see? Why did even the smartest and most experienced scientists agree there was no life out there in space? Chase knew for a fact that there definitely *was* life out in space. Not just creatures, but plants, and machines, and colors that were alive.

As much as Chase wanted to go back to the telescope, he was scared for the first time. He was so sure of his power to see real things in space, things that other people couldn't see. That made him feel different and unsettled. He just wanted to go to bed and try to forget about it all for a bit. He crawled into his bed and slept soundly all night.

The next day, the morning sun greeted Chase as his eyes slowly opened. He looked at the ceiling above him. The stick-on glow-in-the-dark stars above his bed triggered memories from the night before. The girl!

Chase sat up in bed and rubbed his eyes.

Glimpses of the girl dropping her books flashed before

him. Just then, Bogey and Brinkley ran into his room and

up onto his bed. His dogs always had stinky breath and

smiles on their faces. Brinkley was a big, yellow Labrador

puppy. Bogey was an older chocolate Labrador. They

both stood over Chase, licking his cheeks, indicating they

were ready for him to get up and play.

Chase quickly washed his face, brushed his teeth,

and threw on some clothes from his dresser drawers. He

made his way downstairs. Mom must have already left for

the grocery store because the house was unusually quiet.

He knew she always liked to get her grocery shopping

done for the week on Sunday mornings. She liked to meal

prep while watching cooking shows and dancing around

the kitchen. But for the moment, the kitchen was eerily

quiet. Chase didn't like it. He grabbed his iPad and pulled

up his playlist.

He was jamming to his music and slurping down Fruity Pebbles when the door from the garage to the kitchen opened. Mom entered with her arms full of grocery bags. Chase placed his spoon in his bowl. He knew it meant that his cereal might get a little too soggy, but he got up to help Mom with the rest of the groceries anyway. They were able to unload the trunk in no time at all. He sat back down to his fruity cereal and was pleasantly surprised with the crunch in the late bite.

As Mom put the groceries away in the refrigerator and pantry, she asked Chase what he was going to do with his Sunday. He honestly didn't know. He had basketball tryouts later in the day, but he had six hours of freedom before that. He pondered his options while he walked his bowl over to the kitchen sink. Maybe he could ask Jackson to come play. Or he could take his bike out and wander around the new neighborhood to see if he could discover anything cool. He had been thinking about that path and fort that Jackson mentioned.

He opted for taking his bike out. He opened the door to the garage and yelled over his shoulder to his mom that he'd be out on his bike.

"Have fun, honey!" she answered.

Chase pulled his bike off the hook on the wall and settled it onto the cool garage floor. Just hopping on that seat and cruising down the driveway gave him a sense of his old self. His happy self. He turned right at the bottom of the driveway and peddled up the street. He took another right and glided down road, looking at the houses around him. They weren't like the houses in Georgia. They weren't better or worse; they were just different. He kept his eyes out for signs of other kids. He saw another street coming up on his right. He decided on a whim to turn and check it out. As soon as Chase had cleared the curve, his heart sank.

There was a big group of kids playing kickball straight ahead. As much as he wanted to see signs of kids, he wasn't ready for a huge group. But it was too late to turn around. Just as he had seen them, they saw him.

"Hey, that's the new kid," someone shouted.

"I didn't know there was a new kid. What grade is he in?" another kid asked.

"I know him! Hey, Chase! Come here, man," a familiar voice shouted.

Chase knew that was Nick's voice. Chase faked a smile and rode his bike up to the group.

"Hey guys," he said. "You playing kickball?"

What a dumb question! Why did he say that?! Of course they were playing kickball. Duh! Chase wanted to climb under a rock.

But then another voice spoke up. "Yeah, we just started. Want to join?"

Chase scanned the group, only to realize it was Janessa who'd spoken. That couldn't be the same girl who was so rude to him the first day of school. But it was. She gave him a shy smile and Chase smiled back.

"Sure. Game on," Chase agreed.

They all ran toward the center of the street to reassign teams. Chase was pleasantly surprised when he was picked in the second round. Alright. The game got started and Chase's team was in the outfield first. Nick kicked the ball for the other team. It bounced once, right in front of Chase. His quick instincts set in and he grabbed the ball, tossing it accurately to first base. Janessa caught it and tagged Nick right before he could touch the base.

Chase's team cheered, giving each other high fives and jumping up and down. Chase gave the third baseman a fist bump and looked up to see Nick glaring at him. Chase's smile quickly faded. Shoot. He hadn't thought about the repercussions of getting Nick out. He was just playing the game. Although he didn't really like Nick, he certainly didn't want him as an enemy. What was the saying? Keep your friends close and your enemies closer. He was really regretting that last play.

Chase was hesitant to make any other plays against Nick's team for the next few minutes. He really didn't want to start any trouble with anyone. But the more he thought about it, the more he realized that Nick didn't get to control him. He had just as much of a right to be out there playing as anyone else. Chase picked up his game and didn't think about Nick for the rest of the innings.

Nick's team ended up winning 12–10. As competitive as Chase was, he didn't mind this loss. Maybe Nick wouldn't hold such a grudge now that his team had claimed the win. Besides, Chase had fun with the rest of the kids. It reminded him of the days in his old neighborhood in Georgia.

The group of kids was dispersing. Chase picked up his bicycle and jumped on, ready to head back home. He was only a few pedals in when he saw Jackson riding his bike toward him. They met and hit their brakes.

"Shoot. I missed the kickball game, didn't I?" Jackson asked.

"Yeah, we just finished. What have you been up to?" Chase asked.

"Oh, I had to watch my brother," Jackson replied. "My parents are real estate agents, and they have to show houses most weekends. My brother has some disabilities, so even though he's older than me, I had to be there to help him," Jackson said, looking at Chase for a reaction.

Chase didn't know what type of reaction Jackson anticipated, but he said the only thing that came to mind.

"That's cool. You didn't miss much anyway."

The two friends rode their bikes and hung out for the rest of the afternoon. Chase knew he had to be back by 4:00 p.m. for his basketball tryouts. Right before Chase and Jackson went back to their own homes, Chase said, "Are you trying out for basketball today?"

"Yeah, are you?" Jackson asked.

"I am. What's it like, tryouts? In Georgia, we didn't have to try out. The coaches just took all the kids who signed up and split them into even teams."

Jackson shook his head. "Not here, man. There are so many kids that play basketball. They've gotta make some cuts. But you'll be fine. You have more skills than anybody I've played with. I hope we're on the same team.

Wouldn't that be cool?" Jackson asked with a smile.

"Yeah, that would be cool," Chase agreed.

Maybe Chase was getting used to his new town in

Maryland after all.

# 12 HIT THE GROUND

Chase rode his bike back home, up his driveway, and into the garage. He hung his bike on the hook next to the others and headed in the door that led to the kitchen.

"Mom, Dad? I'm home. I'm ready to head to tryouts," Chase called. Bogey and Brinkley came running to greet him.

"Okay, bud. Make a water bottle and jump in the

car. I'm on my way down," Dad hollered from upstairs.

Chase grabbed a water bottle from the drawer in the kitchen and then searched around for the matching top. When he found one, he filled the bottle with water from the sink, screwed the top on, and went out to the car.

Dad climbed in the driver's seat and they were off.

"You ready for this, Chase?" Dad asked from the front of the family SUV. He looked at Chase in the rearview mirror.

"I think I am. I talked to Jackson about tryouts, and I feel pretty good," Chase answered truthfully.

"All you can do is go out there and do your thing. Try your best and show them what you've got," Dad said with a smile. And that's exactly what Chase planned to do.

Tryouts were held at Tatem's middle school. Chase had only been there once for her orientation, but he remembered where the gym was. He walked into the noisy gymnasium and found the check-in desk. The woman checking players in found his name in alphabetical order on the list. The list was longggg. Chase figured there were about fifty kids just in his age group. He wondered how many teams there would be.

Then Chase heard his name called.

"Chase! Hey, Chase! I didn't know you were trying out," Nick yelled as he made his way over.

Oh boy. Chase was hoping to run into Jackson but hadn't thought about the possibility of Nick being there. He didn't want to be rude, but he really wanted to keep his distance from Nick.

"Hey Nick. Yeah, I'm trying out. Have you played for this league before?" Chase asked.

"Oh yeah, I play every year. All the coaches want me on their teams. I don't know why I even need to come to tryouts," he said. Chase thought he could actually see Nick's chest puffing out of his jersey.

"Well, I guess you don't need me wishing you luck then," Chase said with a forced smile. "Have fun out there."

A whistle blew, echoing in the large gym. All the kids listened as coaches called out names for tryouts. They explained this would just be for evaluations and didn't mean you were on that coach's team for the season. Chase listened intently until he heard his name.

Chase ran over and joined a group of guys surrounding a tall, friendly-faced coach. The coach ran through what the kids would be asked to do. Dribbling, passing, shooting. Chase could handle that.

Chase went out there and did his thing. He didn't make every shot, but he made most of them. His passes were clean, and he was able to dribble between the cones without knocking them over. Once, while he was waiting for his turn, he noticed Nick on the other side of the court taking shots too far out and missing.

When his tryout was complete, he met his dad on the sidelines. Chase took a swig from his water bottle and asked, "So, what did you think?" He valued his dad's honest opinions.

"I thought you looked great out there, buddy. Any coach would be lucky to have you on their team," he said with conviction. Hearing that made Chase feel good.

"Alright, we're ready to call teams," someone said into a microphone. All the coaches went out to the middle of the court. "On Coach Duffy's team... Caden, Westin, Jackson, Carson, Jordan, Javon, Preston, Chase, Dylan, and Cam."

Chase's heart fluttered. Chase! He'd made a team. He ran to join the other guys. Jackson was out there too.

The two friends gave each other a fist bump and a hug.

The man with the microphone continued calling out names until all the coaches' teams were filled. He thanked everyone for coming and encouraged anyone who didn't make a team to keep practicing and try out again next year.

It was then that Chase saw Nick up against the gymnasium wall. He didn't make a team. After all that hype, he wasn't selected. Chase watched as Nick's dad yelled at him. His dad's face was red with anger, and Nick looked like he might cry. It didn't make Chase feel good to see this. Even though Nick had made some poor choices, Chase felt bad that his dad was being so hard on him.

Chase's own dad put his arm around him, and they headed home.

After dinner, Chase's mom wanted to go through his backpack and get organized for the week. He pulled everything out of his Friday Folder. As his mom glanced over his papers, his mind was only on one thing. He hadn't thought much about his telescope while he was out playing all day, but now he couldn't wait to get up to his room. As soon as his backpack was cleared out and ready for the week ahead, Mom told him to go take a shower and start getting ready for bed.

"Even though it's Sunday, it's a school night. I'll be up to tuck you in in a bit," Mom said.

As soon as Chase got up to his room, he shut his door. He wasn't allowed to lock it, but shutting it gave him the privacy he desired. Chase walked toward his telescope and took a seat. He couldn't resist the urge to see more. He squinted one eye and looked through the viewfinder with his other. He didn't have to turn the focus knob at all this time. There was a sharp view on exactly what he was looking for.

There she was: this purple creature that pulled at his heartstrings and made him want to know more. She was doing something with the flowers. It looked like she was petting them and talking to them. Wow, this place was strange.

Out of the corner of his eye, Chase could see the group of kids that had knocked her down heading her way. They were laughing and pointing as they approached. Chase's heart sank. This girl didn't deserve to be bullied again. He didn't know what it was about her, but he felt a connection to her. Her eyes told the truth— that she was one of the good ones. As he looked through the telescope, he wished with all his might that the whole pack of kids would just fall down and leave her alone.

Slam! The group of kids hit the ground hard.
They all looked at each other in confusion. They got up
and ran the other direction, unsure of what had just taken
place, but knowing they had to get out of there.

Chase's heart felt like it had stopped beating. He
had to remind himself to breathe. Did he just make those
kids fall? He had clearly wished that they would fall and
leave her alone, and that's exactly what happened. He
looked back into the telescope. She was standing there,
looking just as confused as the other kids had looked, and
she was staring right at Chase.

# 13 I CAN HEAR YOU

Chase had had enough for one night. In the past two

days, he had confirmed that he could see life in space. He

had seen a whole other working society and learned that

he might even be able to control some of the creatures'

actions with his own thoughts. He didn't like how he had

made that group of mean creatures fall to the ground, but

he knew, without a doubt, that he'd controlled that whole

situation. It couldn't have been a coincidence that they fell right at the same time he wished it. Or could it? Chase took a shower and climbed into bed. The shower had relaxed him. He lay in bed trying to get sleepy but wondering what he had gotten himself into.

Chase's mom and dad came up and knocked on his door.

"Come in," he told them. They entered with smiles. Mom gazed around his room, clearly checking to see if he had been keeping it tidy. Her not saying anything meant he passed her test. Dad came to Chase's bedside and turned his attention to the telescope next to them.

"How's it working for you, bud?" he asked. Chase's dad had been calling him "bud" for as long as he could remember.

"Good. I think I found some of the stuff Mrs.

Ross showed me at the picnic. I know I found Jupiter," Chase said. He didn't want to tell him the details, but he didn't want to lie either.

Chase's dad nodded. "Pretty cool," he said, looking out the window. Chase's parents said goodnight and turned out the light as they left his room. Chase stared up at the star stickers glowing on his ceiling until he finally drifted off. Chase slept long and hard.

The next week was uneventful at school. Chase was starting to feel more comfortable walking through the halls. Every face he saw was no longer strange. He started recognizing his teachers and a few of his classmates. Sometimes kids would wave or smile, but mostly they just kept walking by. Chase no longer felt like an invisible ghost, but he didn't feel completely at home either.

He was glad when the week was over. Chase said, "Have a good weekend," to Ms. Linda as he got off the bus on Friday, ready for a weekend of no homework and lots of relaxation. Ms. Linda had reached out to him on his first day and kept talking to him each day after. He liked her. He walked down the sidewalk past three houses until he turned up his driveway. Bogey and Brinkley were in the backyard. When they saw Chase, they came running up to the fence, barking and wagging their tails. It made Chase happy to see them so excited to greet him. "Hey, you two," Chase said as he reached through the fence to give them head rubs. When he walked through the garage door into the kitchen, Chase could smell Mom's homemade spaghetti sauce. Yum!

"Hey, Chase," Mom said with a big smile. "How was your day?"

"Ah, it was alright. Nothing great, nothing awful. Just a regular day."

Mom replied, "Well, how about we change that? Let's make this day great! Want to go out for ice cream after dinner? Just you and me?"

"Sure," Chase said. "I'm never going to turn down an invitation for ice cream. Thanks, Mom!"

Chase hung his backpack on the hooks in the mudroom and washed his hands. He grabbed a banana and filled Mom in a little more about his day. Then he headed up to his room to chill.

As soon as he entered his room, Chase saw the telescope. Truth be told, he noticed that telescope every time he walked in his room. He told himself he would not look through it during the week. For one, he needed a break to see if this was real or all in his head. Two, he really did need to focus on his schoolwork and making friends. As curious as he was about that telescope, Chase resisted the urge to peek during the school week.

But it was officially the weekend, right? Chase thought about it and told himself he would wait until dark that night.

He jumped into his beanbag chair and grabbed his remote. Chase joined a game and slipped into an alternate universe with his videogaming friends.

He must have been playing for over an hour because before he knew it, the dinner bell was ringing. Chase turned off his game and headed downstairs.

Chase could smell the spaghetti and garlic bread before he could see it. It was one of his favorite meals. Chase was in a great mood as he slid into his chair.

Dad started the conversation. "Well, Mom and I have some exciting news."

The things that went through Tatem and Chase's heads! They thought of everything- moving back to Georgia, a new baby, moving somewhere completely different, putting in a pool, going on vacation, someone visiting, or a family cleaning day.

"What is it, Dad?" Chase asked cautiously.

Mom and Dad looked at each other and smiled.

"Oh, c'mon! What's going on?" Tatem pressed.

"Your dad and I have been talking. We know this move has been hard on both of you. We are so proud of the way you've put your best foot forward and adjusted to our new life in Maryland," Mom said.

Dad continued, "So, we thought we would reward

you two with a day in North Carolina with some of your friends from Georgia. It's halfway, so they'll drive a few hours north, we'll drive a few hours south, and we'll get a chance to visit and reconnect at one of the world's best amusement parks. What do you think about that?" Dad asked with a sparkle in his eye.

Chase and Tatem both squealed with excitement and got up to hug their parents. Even though they were getting used to Maryland, they missed their old friends. The Magnussons spent the rest of dinner gobbling up the delicious meal and going over the details for the trip. Chase's heart was light and happy.

After dinner, Dad took Tatem to meet up with some of her new friends, while Mom made good on the promise she'd made to Chase about an ice cream date.

Chase picked an ice cream shop that his bus

passed each day. He had always wondered what it was like. They pulled up and parked the car in the gravel lot.

As they walked into the shop, Chase wondered if they had any fun specialty flavors. The smell of cold cream and sugar wafted through the air. His eyes went right to the menu board. Lavender Honey, Cap'n Crunch, Bubble Gum, Cherry Chocolate, and Mint Green Monster Cookie all stood out to Chase. He decided on Bubble Gum and his mom picked Cherry Chocolate. They put their orders in with the teenager behind the counter and went to look for seats.

Chase scanned the tables in the little shop and saw Janessa sitting with two women. She was looking at him and eating a rainbow sherbet cone. Chase didn't know which Janessa he was going to get tonight. She had been so mean the first day of school. But then she was nice when she included him in the kickball game. He decided he would be friendly and give her a smile. She smiled back.

"Who's that, Chase?" Mom whispered, trying not to let Janessa's table hear her.

"She goes to my school. I think she might live in our neighborhood too," Chase said quietly.

Mom smiled at the table of ladies. Then she started walking toward their table. Chase froze. What was she doing?

"Hi, I'm Michelle Magnusson, Chase's mom," she explained as she stuck out her hand to introduce herself. "We just moved here not too long ago. It looks like our kiddos know each other from school."

The other two women matched her smile. "Oh, it's so nice to meet you. I'm Tori and this is Liz. We're Janessa's moms," they said as they each shook Mom's hand.

The grown-ups stood and talked for a minute.
Chase was completely embarrassed that his mom had
approached them. He just wanted to vanish. Then he
looked at Janessa. She was no longer happily eating her
ice cream cone. She was looking away and seemed
uncomfortable. Without thinking, he walked over to her.

"Hey, Janessa," Chase said casually. He hoped talking to her would make her feel better somehow. She got up out of her seat and headed to the trash can. Chase followed her.

As Janessa dropped her cone in the wastebasket, Chase asked, "Is everything okay?"

Janessa answered Chase in a whisper. "Don't you have something to say about me having two moms?"

The question took Chase aback. He didn't know many people that had two moms or two dads, but he certainly wasn't going to say that to Janessa. He was a little insulted that Janessa took him for someone who would judge her like that.

"No. I don't have anything to say about it. Your moms seem really nice," he said. They both looked over at the table, where the three women were laughing about who knows what.

"If there's anything to talk about, it's that my mom thinks it's okay to chat with everyone she meets like they've known each other for years. Your moms are nice to speak with her," Chase continued.

"Thanks," Janessa said with a smile. It made Chase sad to think about why Janessa had asked him that. Had other people confronted her about her parents? He hoped not, but he was worried that she had dealt with some mean people in the past.

The teenager behind the counter called out their order, and Chase went to grab his and his mom's ice creams. They sat with Janessa's family. He ended up getting to know her better and having a good time.

When they all left, Chase's mom exchanged contact information with Janessa's moms. As they climbed into the car, she said, "Well they are certainly a nice family." Chase smiled, thinking how lucky he was to have parents that were so friendly and genuinely accepting of everyone.

When they got home, Chase went up to his room while his parents read together on the living room couches. He knew they would be engulfed in their stories and wouldn't interrupt him if he looked through his telescope.

Chase sat in the chair by his window, took a deep breath, and looked through the lens. It didn't take long for him to find the now familiar faraway land. His eye focused in on the colorful shops that lined the streets. He tried reading the signs, but the letters did not look like English letters. They looked like 3D cursive, but not the kind of cursive his third-grade teacher had taught him. It was new. He stared at one sign and, inexplicably, he was able to read it! It read, "Galaxy Ice Cream." How in the world did he just read this space writing? His reading was confirmed when he saw two space creatures walk out the door with ice cream cones. How ironic that he had just gone for ice cream himself.

He tried looking for the familiar girl but couldn't find her. After a few minutes of looking, he decided to call it a night. Chase brushed his teeth, turned out his lights, and drifted to sleep.

Chase woke unusually early Saturday morning. It was still dark. The things he had seen in the telescope were the first thoughts that popped in his mind. He hadn't even wiped the sleepies from his eyes and he was already juggling feelings of excitement and confusion.

Chase was torn. He desperately wanted to share all this information with someone. He wanted to tell someone about the girl, the ice cream shop, the roller-coasters, the way he made the mean kids fall. All of it. At the same time, he knew it was a very risky move to tell anyone any of this. He would sound absolutely absurd! And besides, *who* would he even tell anyway?

All his friends back in Georgia would think he was full of bologna. He wondered if they missed him and still thought of him, or if he was completely forgotten yet. Knowing that he'd see them in North Carolina in a few weeks settled his nerves. He tried to think of someone he could talk to here in Maryland.

Jackson? He liked Jackson and all, but their friendship was new, and he certainly didn't want to scare him away. Heck, Jackson was one of the only friends Chase had here. Janessa? Maybe, but their friendship was just starting. If he told her, she might call him *strange*.

There was no way he was going to tell Nick. That was totally out of the question. There was something about Nick that made Chase feel slimy and icky. He didn't like the way he lied at the picnic to that volunteer. He didn't like how he was just trying to beat the system. Chase wasn't about to trust Nick with anything.

Could he tell his sister, Tatem? Usually he felt like he could tell her anything. But, with this information, he was pretty sure she would think his imagination was getting away from him. Besides, Tatem was too busy trying to make new friends and get her own life up and going in Maryland. This move couldn't have been easy for her either. This was the first time that Chase stopped and thought about that. He had been feeling so sorry for himself with the move, and then felt all this excitement with the telescope, but he really hadn't stopped to think about how Tatem was doing. She was a good big sister, always looking out for Chase. Maybe it was time he started looking out for her. He would start today by not bothering her with this crazy news.

Mom was not a possibility. That was a hard no. She would be so worried with Chase's stories that she would probably make a doctor's appointment. He was not signing up for that!

Hmmm. What about Dad? Dad was a little cryptic when he left him with the telescope. Chase remembered him saying, "Be careful. Space is a very mysterious place. It has the power to pull you in." Maybe his dad would understand. Heck, maybe he even knew about this other world. Chase thought it through. Out of all those choices, maybe Dad would be the best person to talk to.

Then it hit him. He could try to talk to the space creature! If he could control the mean kids' actions, why couldn't he try to talk with the girl out in space? She had looked right at him. He felt a strange connection to her too. Who was he kidding? The connection to her wasn't the only strange thing in this situation. The entire situation was strange!

Chase climbed out of his bed and went to brush his teeth. If he was going to try to talk with her, he certainly didn't need to have morning breath. He reached for his toothbrush and plopped on a gob of ocean blue toothpaste. He brushed up and down, side to side, and even gave his tongue a quick skim with his toothbrush. Chase stood in front of the mirror and took a hard look at himself. He felt like he looked a little older than last time he checked the mirror. His face looked a little more defined. He washed his face too, just for good measure. His bedhead was a lost cause. He tossed some water on his hair and roughly ran a brush through it. Good enough.

Chase ran over to his bedroom window. He pulled the chair out a little, sat back down and thought, *Here goes nothing*. He drew in a deep breath and let it out slowly. He squinted one eye and used the other to look through the viewfinder. Because he hadn't moved a thing on his telescope, he was able to focus right in on the same scene from last night. He squinted harder and saw the familiar buildings, bright and vibrant in color. He saw the strange flowers, and this time they were absolutely talking to each other. There were creatures walking, working, talking, and going about their days. But he didn't see her.

Then a magenta door to a lime green house opened. Chase turned his telescope ever so slightly to zoom in on the house. She came strolling out with a peaceful look on her face. Chase noticed her pink cheeks, high on the sides of her face. He noticed her small button nose and smooth lips that looked like they could crack into a smile quite easily. She had shoulder-length hair, but her hair was much thicker than humans here on Earth. Her hair was as thick as ropes of licorice. She was wearing a dress, but not like the fancy dresses Mom made Tatem wear to church on Christmas Eve. No, this dress looked cool and flowy. She looked very comfortable as she walked down the front path from her door.

Chase immediately had second thoughts about talking to her. Heck, he didn't even know if he *could* talk to her. What if she didn't speak his language? What if he scared her? Okay, okay. What did he have to lose? He cleared his throat a little, and in a voice louder than a whisper but not quite as loud as his usual speaking voice, he said, "Excuse me. Can you hear me?"

The girl stopped in her tracks. She slowly turned her head as she searched all around her. Then her eyes met his. For a moment she stared right at Chase, and without saying a word, she nodded.

# 14 THE FIRST UNIVERSAL CONNECTOR

Chase was floored. There was no question now. This girl could hear him alright. He had so many questions.

"What is your name?" Chase asked the girl. He could barely believe the question had squeaked out of his mouth. He was dumbstruck.

"Palunga," she answered, still looking right at Chase. Now that was a name Chase had never heard ore. Not once had there been a Palunga in any of his

lasses. Not in Georgia, not in Maryland. He was thirsty

to learn more.

"What is the name of your land?" he asked.

"Callisto," the girl answered in a sweet, soft voice.

"I live here with my family. It is a moon of Jupiter. I can't

believe I'm actually talking with you."

Then she continued, "You must be Chase from planet Earth."

Chase's heart felt like it was in his throat. It was beating so fast. He couldn't answer her. How in the world did she know who he was and where he lived?

"Um, yes. I am Chase. How did you know?" he finally asked.

"Oh, don't tell me you don't know. We have all been waiting for you. I have been waiting for you," she said with a smile.

Chase drew in another deep breath. "Me?" he asked her. "Why me?"

"Everyone on every planet and every moon knows of you, Chase. You are the son of Matthew, The Universal Connector," Palunga said very matter-of-factly.

Chase absorbed this information and thought for a moment. He had never heard of "The Universal Connector." It sounded cool, though, and important. Hmmm. Matthew, The Universal Connector. Was that his father? Well, Chase's dad *was* named Matt. But it still couldn't be right. Chase's dad was just a normal dad. He was goofy, told bad dad jokes, worked hard, played golf, coached Little League lacrosse teams. He certainly was not a Universal Connector! No, there had to be some mistake.

"No, I'm not who you think I am. I'm just Chase from Georgia and now Maryland. I have never heard of The Universal Connector. I'm just a regular kid. You've got me all wrong."

"Chase, it's true. I'm sorry. I thought you knew all of this," Palunga continued. "Matthew hasn't spoken to any of us in years. After you and your sister were born, he said he had to focus on his earthly family. He told us to be kind to one another and that one day, one of his children would come forth to be the next Connector. I just figured you knew all this."

Chase's brain was processing this new information as quickly as it could, but it was still so much to wrap his head around. Maybe she was right. His dad had said he used to study astronomy in college. And his dad did warn him that space is very mysterious. Chase knew what he had to do next.

"Thank you, Palunga. I will be back to visit you soon." And with that, Chase pushed his chair back and ran out of his room.

# 15 A LETTER FROM DAD

"Dad! Dad! Where are you? I need to talk to you," Chase

yelled frantically as he ran down the stairs.

His mom was sitting on the couch, sipping coffee

with music playing quietly in the background. "Good

morning, honey. You're up early," she said.

"Mom, I really just need to talk to Dad. Where is

he?" Chase asked anxiously.

"Your father is on the golf course. He told me you might be looking for him though. I don't know what this is all about, but he left a letter for you on the counter."

"Thanks, Mom." Chase barely got the words out as he dashed to the kitchen.

On the counter was a letter, sealed in an envelope, with "My Buddy, Chase" written across the front.

Chase was about to pick it up when a hand swept in and grabbed it.

"What do we have here?" Tatem sang, looking at the letter in her hand. She was up early for a tennis lesson.

"Oh no you don't!" Chase said. He jumped up and snagged the letter out of Tatem's hands before she en knew what he was doing.

"Get back here! Mom, Chase is up to something!" Tatem yelled.

But Chase didn't hear any more of it. He had the letter in his hands and was running as fast as he could. Where could he go? He needed a spot where no one would bother him. He remembered that Jackson had told him about a fort. It was at the end of the trail in the woods. Chase was outside before he knew it, running down the driveway and around the corner. He ran so fast down the hill that he felt like he was flying over the sidewalk. He ran to the opening into the woods, where the grass met the trees that spread apart for the trail. Chase followed the path all the way, trusting what his new friend had told him. Sure enough, at the end of the path, there was a fort.

The fort was pretty much a big wooden box that
stood out from the lush trees. It wasn't much, but it had
four wooden walls and a dirt floor. There was no door,
just a sawed-out opening that Chase walked through.
Once inside, Chase sat in the corner and stared at the
letter. His breath was loud and labored. He could smell
the earth and damp grass around him. He peeled the
corner back and opened the seal of the envelope. He

pulled out a single sheet of paper. His dad's handwriting was all over it. It read,

Dear Chase,

If you are reading this, I assume you must have had quite a night looking through your telescope. I am sure you are looking for an explanation, so I will try my best.

When I studied astronomy in college, I realized that I could see a lot more than my classmates. I could see life in space, something no one else has been able to see. I tried to explain it to my professor, but he thought I was just pulling his leg. No one else could see what I could see, even when they were looking through the same exact telescope at the same exact setting.

One day, accidentally, I noticed that the space creatures could see and hear me, just as I could see and hear them. They knew I was the only one that could do this on Earth, so they asked me if I could reach out to other creatures on other planets and moons. I did, and I helped creatures communicate all over the universe.

...t is how I got my title, "The Universal Connector."

I felt an obligation to the world. It was a huge responsibility. I was trying to live my best life here on Earth, but I wanted to help everyone else in the whole universe as well. Once I married your mom and we had you and your sister, I knew I had to step back. Being a father is the most important job in the world, one that I do not take lightly. I knew that if I was going to be a good dad, I had to be fully present in your lives. That meant giving up my space communication.

I had an inkling that one day, one of my children would own the same powers as me. You confirmed that suspicion when I came across "LIFE ON JUPITER MOON" in the search history on my laptop. I had no doubt what you were up to. It takes a very special person to be able to see past the impossible and see what could be. You possess all the qualities that a true Connector must have. You have empathy for others. You fight for fairness in all situations. You know how important it is to feel love nd friendship, and also how hard it is to feel alone in this world.

Chase, you are the new "Universal Connector." It is up to you what you do with that title. I trust you. I look forward to hearing all about your adventures.

See you this afternoon.

Love,

Dad

# 16 A NEW UNIVERSAL CONNECTOR

Chase sat there with the letter in his hands for a long
time.

He thought about the times when he had done
the right thing—the thing that his conscience told him to
do. He had stood up for the little girl who dropped her
books in the school field. He didn't cheat at the duck
game. He spoke up in the basketball game for what was

nt. But he didn't know that it really mattered to anyone in particular, much less to the whole universe.

He finally stood up, put the letter in his pocket, and walked slowly down the path back to his new home.

He was deep in thought the whole way home. If others thought he was capable of being The Connector of the Universe, he could certainly handle this move. He made a vow to himself, right then and there, that he would try harder. He would talk to the kids at the bus stop. He would invite Jackson over to play more. He would look up with confidence in the hallways at school. He would continue to stick up for what was right in a way that didn't put others down.

When Chase got home, he ran up to his room with his letter. He tucked it in his bottom desk drawer before Tatem could follow him in to see what was up. It didn't take long for her to show up at his door.

"What's going on in here?" she demanded. She came right in and hopped on his bed. "I know something is up."

Chase didn't know the right words to explain it all in that moment. Instead, he just said, "I don't know. I think I've just learned a lot about myself through this move. Everything was so easy back in Georgia. It hasn't been easy here, but I think I'm finally realizing that this move was good for me. I feel like myself again, maybe even better. I just want to be my true self." Chase looked up at his sister.

"I know what you mean," she said back to him.
"It hasn't been easy being new. It's lonely. It's hard. It
makes you really think about the kind of friend you want
to be and the kind of friends you want to have. I've met
some nice kids. I just don't have the history with them,
like I had with all my old friends."

"But you will," Chase assured her. "It just takes
time. The more you are your authentic self, the more

people will gravitate to you. Trust me."

Tatem smiled. "When did you get so wise, little brother? One minute you're crawling around in diapers and the next minute you're giving me life advice," she teased. "But I'll take it. You're absolutely right."

Tatem leaned in and gave Chase a hug. It felt good to be on the same page as her. They were going to be fine.

Tatem told Chase she had to run and check her phone. She was pretty sure she was going to meet up with some friends at that ice cream shop he had gone to with Mom. He told her to have fun as she left his room.

Chase moseyed over to the chair and telescope. It wasn't dark yet. He wouldn't be able to see anything, even if he tried. But he sat there for a minute, dusting the telescope off with the edge of his T-shirt.

He was The Universal Connector. The galaxy believed in him, and he believed in himself.

Chase felt invincible. It just took stepping out of his reality for a moment to realize his full potential.

# ABOUT THE AUTHOR

Laura Coy is a teacher, writer, and lifelong learner. Laura has written for *The Examiner* as the family and parenting editor. She also has a memoir published in *Tales2Inspire, The Moonstone Collection,* created by Lois W. Stern.

This is her debut novel, written from the inspiration of some of her third-grade students, who struggled finding a book to connect to. The plot stemmed from a dream she had about her family. Laura recently created Enchanted Moon Press, where she looks forward to publishing many more stories for young readers.

Laura lives outside of Atlanta, Georgia, with her husband, Matt. They have two children, Tatem and Chase, two dogs, but no, they do not talk to space creatures in real life.

You can find Laura online at www.enchantedmoonpress.com and @Lauracoywrites.

## A WORD BY THE AUTHOR:

If you enjoyed this book, it would be very appreciated if you could take a short minute to leave a lovely review on Amazon. Your kind and honest feedback is so very important to me. It gives me, the author, encouragement for bad days when I want to throw in the towel and blast off to Callisto! Thank you so very much for your time!

To keep up with Enchanted Moon Press, please visit our website.